For Helen, Martin and Katie
with love
~*PB*

For Isobel, William, Catherine and Lizzie
with love
~*BC*

LITTLE TIGER PRESS
An imprint of Magi Publications
1 The Coda Centre, 189 Munster Road, London SW6 6AW
www.littletigerpress.com

First published in Great Britain 2003

Text © Paul Bright 2003 • Illustrations © Ben Cort 2003
Paul Bright and Ben Cort have asserted their rights to be identified as the author and illustrator
of this work under the Copyright, Designs and Patents Act, 1988 • All rights reserved
ISBN 1 85430 863 7

A CIP catalogue record for this book is available from the British Library

Printed in Belgium by Proost

1 3 5 7 9 10 8 6 4 2

Paul Bright Ben Cort

bed

Little Tiger Press
London

Under the bed there's a smelly shoe,
A piece of jigsaw, green and blue,
Some purple pants, an apple core

. . . but under the bed there's

something more!

Under the bed there are bugs and beasts, nibbling crumbs for their

midnight feasts, gobbling, squabbling, all night through, And much too busy to think about you.

Under the bed is a dragon dozing,
One eye closed, the other closing,
Dreaming of mountains and morning dew,
And much too sleepy to think about you.

Under the bed is an alligator,
Who might be feeling hungry later.
He likes a pizza, or maybe two,
So I don't expect he'll be bothering you.

Under the bed is a grizzly bear
(Now, don't ask me how he got there),
Rolling and scratching, like grizzlies do,
And far too lazy to think about you.

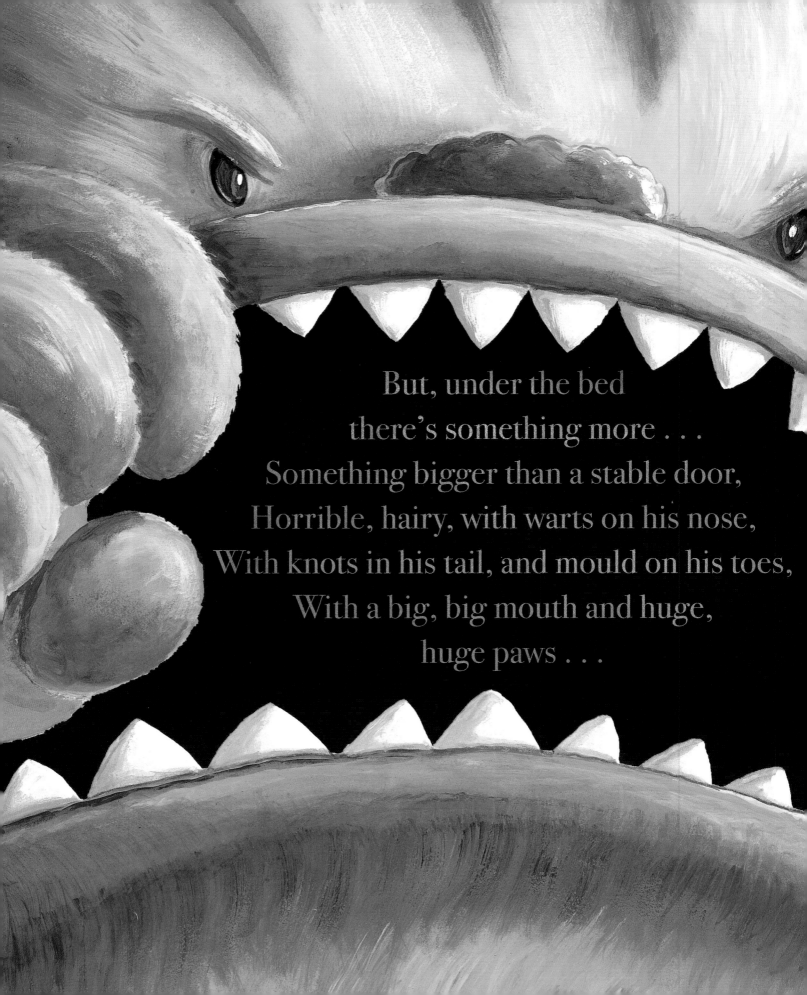

But, under the bed
there's something more . . .
Something bigger than a stable door,
Horrible, hairy, with warts on his nose,
With knots in his tail, and mould on his toes,
With a big, big mouth and huge,
huge paws . . .

. . . though he's never been
known to show his claws.

He's under the bed
and he's sucking his thumb!
He calls for his daddy
or mummy to come!
And he says as he shakes
from his toes to his head:

"I saw something frightening inside the bed!"

And out of the room flee the bugs and beasts,
Scattering crumbs from their midnight feasts.
Out of the room flies the dragon dozing,
One eye open and the other one closing.

Out of the room crawls the alligator,
Who might be feeling hungry later.
Out of the room bounds the grizzly bear
(And don't ask me how he got there).

And out of the room runs something more,
Who trips on his tail as he gets to the door,
Who rolls down the stairs falling flat on his nose,
Bashing his bottom and banging his toes,
With a big, big mouth and huge, huge paws . . .
though he never showed even a glimpse
of his claws.
They all run out in a terrible stew,
For the frightening thing in the bed is . . .

YOU!

Now there's nobody under the bed any more. But you'd better just look, to be perfectly sure!